CHARLIE AND THE PRESCHOOL PRODIGAL

by Ginger M. Blomberg

illustrated by Samara Hardy

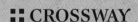

CROSSWAY

WHEATON, ILLINOIS

Gige M. Blomberg

11/10/24 S.D.G.

Library of Congress Cataloging-in-Publication Data

Names: Blomberg, Ginger, 1980– author. | Hardy, Samara, illustrator.

Title: Charlie and the preschool prodigal / by Ginger Blomberg ; illustrated by Samara Hardy.

Description: Wheaton, Illinois : Crossway, [2024] | Series: TGC kids | Audience: Ages 3–7.

Identifiers: LCCN 2022058953 | ISBN 9781433584817 (hardcover)

Subjects: CYAC: Brothers—Fiction. | Family life—Fiction. | Christian life—Fiction. | Parables. | LCGFT: Christian fiction. | Picture books.

Classification: LCC PZ7.1.B6356 Ch 2024 | DDC [E]--dc23

LC record available at https://lccn.loc.gov/2022058953

Crossway is a publishing ministry of Good News Publishers.

RRDS			34	33	32	31	30	29	28	27	26	25	24
15	14	13	12	11	10	9	8	7	6	5	4	3	2	1

"But while he was still a long way off, his father saw him and felt compassion, and ran and embraced him and kissed him."

LUKE 15:20

Eddie could make trouble.

He ate crayons. And ants.

He crashed down the stairs in a cardboard box. He stuck gum to the dining room wall.

He pretended to be a puppy and chewed up his daddy's slippers.

"Eddie is our wild child," Daddy said with a sigh, while Eddie sat
in time-out again.

Eddie had a big brother named Charlie. Charlie liked things to be orderly. He liked people to be orderly, too.

Charlie made his bed every day. He told Eddie to make his own bed. Charlie felt it was important for children to get plenty of sleep, and he often reminded his parents about Eddie's bedtime.

Charlie combed his hair carefully every morning and tried to comb Eddie's hair, but Eddie did not like it.

"Charlie is our tidy child," Daddy said with a sigh, when Charlie told guests to take off their shoes before they came into the house.

One day, Eddie decided to run away.

He packed his lunch box with a piece of string to catch fish in case he got hungry, half a deck of playing cards in case he got bored, his dad's new silk tie in case he needed to look fancy, and two pieces of candy: one that his mother had said he could eat after his afternoon rest and one that belonged to Charlie.

He walked out of the front door and into the neighbors' yard.
The neighbors had a big bush by their house that would
make a good hideout. Eddie climbed in.

In a minute, he heard his daddy walking outside and calling for him. Eddie stayed quiet and hidden. Daddy went back inside. Eddie could still hear him calling in the house, but after a while Eddie stopped listening.

It was fun under the bush. For a few minutes. No one could tell Eddie what to do now. He ate both pieces of candy. He pulled out his cards. He wiped his chin with the smooth, silky tie.

But it wasn't fun for long. Soon, he got a mosquito bite on his ankle and another one on his elbow. After his candy, he was thirsty. And cards were not much fun by himself.

Eddie decided to make himself a bed right there in his hideout so he could be more comfortable. After a lot of work, he put his head down on the small pile of leaves and twigs he had gathered. It did not feel much like his bed at home.

He thought about going home. He wondered if he could walk to a store first to buy a clean tie for his daddy and new candy for his brother. He did not have any money, so he started digging a hole in case there might be some treasure buried under the bush. He found only a white grub and an old dog toy.

So he sat and sat. Eddie remembered that it wasn't safe for kids to go off alone. He missed his family. Did anyone miss him? He thought he heard someone calling his name, but he wasn't sure. He hugged his knees and wondered what he should do.

Then a wasp flew into the bush. It buzzed around Eddie's head, and it landed right on his arm. Suddenly, Eddie knew exactly what to do. He leaped out of the bush and darted back to his house.

Daddy looked through the window and saw Eddie come into the yard. Daddy threw open the door and ran outside.

"Eddie!" he called as he ran to his son. "We were looking everywhere for you! I'm so glad you're safe!" Eddie was dirty. And sticky. And he had leaves in his hair. But Daddy didn't make Eddie clean up first. He grabbed Eddie and wrapped him in a mighty hug. "I called our neighbors to help me look for you," Daddy said. "I was about to call the police!"

"I'm sorry, Daddy," Eddie said in a small voice. He put his arms around his daddy's neck, and Daddy carried his little boy inside.

"Charlie!" Daddy called. "We found Eddie! Come down.
Let's all go out for ice cream!"

Charlie did not come. Charlie did not move. He folded his arms, sat on his bed, and felt angry. Daddy came to him and sat down beside him.

"It's not fair!" Charlie shouted. "Eddie ran away! He took my candy. Why does he get ice cream?"

"Eddie did eat your candy," Daddy said, "and he ruined my new tie. Eddie and I will talk later. I bought those things, and I can replace them. But your brother was missing, and now he's home! I would give more than a hundred ties and a thousand candies to have my son safe with us at home."

Daddy put his arm around Charlie. "Do you know who else is important to me? You are, Charlie. I love you, and I always will. Even though you didn't come when I called, either."

Daddy got up and walked to the door. He turned back to Charlie. "Will you come and celebrate with us?"

What do you think Charlie chose?

What would you choose?

Note to Grown-Ups

THE PARABLE OF THE PRODIGAL SON is found in the Bible in Luke 15:11–32. It is a story about a father and two sons. One son behaves badly and wastes the gifts his father gives him. He apologizes, but he can never really pay back the harm he caused. The other brother serves his father faithfully and works hard, but he thinks all that work has earned him the right to tell the father what to do. Both brothers are invited by their father to a feast, but the story ends without the readers knowing whether the older brother will attend.

The Bible makes it clear that sin has consequences, and sin always has a cost. Jesus did not ignore justice by simply erasing the consequences of sin. Instead, he paid the cost himself by dying on the cross and rising again so that we can be saved. Because of Christ's tremendous love and sacrifice for us, and with the help of the Holy Spirit, we have new freedom and new desire to love Christ and to love others well.

In the story of the prodigal son, the son who leaves and the son who stays *both* need the father's grace. This story is a powerful reminder that we *all* fall short of God's holiness (Rom. 3:23), that God loves us, and that only he can save us (Rom. 5:8–9). Wild children sometimes think they can make life great by doing whatever they want. Tidy children sometimes think they can make life great by working really, really hard.

But the route to real joy is found in our Father's love, which we receive because Christ earned it for us.

Wild children and tidy children, grown-ups who run away and get lost and grown-ups who wear themselves out trying to be right all the time, all need God's grace and can have a seat waiting for them at the feast.